The Cheese

By **Margie Palatini**

Paintings by

Steve Johnson and **Lou Fancher**

KATHERINE TEGEN BOOKS
An Imprint of HarperCollinsPublishers

Rules and Regulations

The cheese stands alone
The cheese stands alone
Hi-ho the dairy-o
The cheese stands alone

SIGH

The rat looked down in the dell and shook his head.
"What a waste of a chunk of cheddar."
He turned to go into his hole—and then he stopped.
He looked back at the cheese standing all alone
in the middle of the meadow.
So yellow. So mellow. . . . So tasty.

This is ridiculous! What's the point of a hunk of cheese being left out and lonesome when it can be enjoying the company of a perfectly fine rat like me?

None that he could think of.
The rat licked his lips, grabbed a napkin, and scurried down the hill for some dinner in the dell.

"And just where do you think you're going?" asked the cat, suddenly jumping down from a tree.

"Me?" answered the surprised rat. "Uh, why . . . just out for a short stroll."

"You don't look like you're strolling," said the cat to the rat. "You look like you're scurrying and sneaking."

SCURRYing and SNEAKing! WeLL!

The rat sounded very insulted. And as he was quite a good actor, he almost convinced the cat that he was indeed out just for a walk. But the cat, who was very clever herself, caught sight of the napkin.

THe Cat's EviDencE

THe NapKiN

ScUrrYiNg

SNeaKiNg

THe cHeesE

"Aha!" she declared with a wave. "And just what is this?"

The rat grumbled. "Oh, if you must know, I'm going to get the cheese."

"The cheese?" said the cat. "You can't do that. Everyone knows the cheese stands alone."

"Give me one good reason why the cheese stands alone."

The cat thought.

"Well . . . umm . . . hrmmmm . . . It's the song," she said. "Yes, it's most definitely the song. The song says, 'The cheese stands alone,' and that's that."

"Well, I think it's a silly song," said the rat, taking back his napkin. "And I'm going to eat that cheese."

The cat looked at the rat. She looked down
in the dell at the cheese.
It *did* look rather lonely.
The cat could not argue that the song was
silly. And as finicky an eater as she was,
the cat did have a fondness for a
nibble of cheese now and then.
"You know, I believe you
may be correct. That cheese
should not stand alone."

The rat smiled and held out a paw.

Care to join me for a bit of cheddar, my dear?

So off went the two, down into the dell, headed for the cheese.

"Calm down and sit," said the cat. "If you must know, we're going to eat the cheese."

"The cheese?" said the dog. "The cheese in the dell? The cheese in the dell? But the cheese stands alone. Everyone knows that."

"Yeah, yeah, yeah. Stop your slobbering," muttered the rat. "We know all about it. But why should good food go to waste because of some silly song?"

The dog thought.
(Which was not an easy thing for him to do.)

He looked across the dell at the cheese. It *did* look very lonely. And, even the dog had to admit, it was a silly song.

"You know," he said with a drool, "I could go for a nosh right about now myself."

So off went the rat, the cat, and the dog to eat the cheese.

That dog can never keep a secret.

The child looked at the dog. She looked down in the dell.

Why, you aren't thinking of eating that cheese, are you? Naughty, naughty puppy. You know the cheese stands alone.

The dog rolled over with a whimper and a whine.

Woof! Arf! Arf! Arf!

The rat moaned. "This is pitiful."
"I'll take care of this," said the cat.

Woof!

Woof!

Meow!

Squeak!

The cat walked up to the child. Purred. Arched. Rubbed. And mewed.

The child giggled. "You know, that piece of cheese *does* look awfully yummy. And I haven't had my afternoon snack. How about you?"

So off went the child, the dog, the cat, and the rat to eat the cheese.

And then . . . Mother called.

Shush.

Shush.

Shush?

"I'm going to eat the cheese," called out the child, who was completely unshushable.

"What a little blabbermouth," muttered the rat.

"No, no, you can't eat the cheese," said Mother. "The cheese stands alone. Wait until your father comes home."

So they all waited for the cow to come home with
the farmer, who was the father, who was told by the
mother that the child wanted to eat the cheese.

The Farmer in the Dell shook his head.

Nope. Can't eat the cheese. CHEESE STANDS ALONE. Everyone knows that.

The wife looked at the child, who looked at the dog, who looked at the cat, who looked at the rat, who looked at the cheese.

It was very quiet until everyone's tummy started to grumble. After a long day's work, the farmer's grumbled the loudest.

"I suppose that song is rather silly," he said, looking down in the dell and staring at the large hunk of cheese.

"It truly is," said his wife.

The farmer took off his hat and scratched his head. "What should we do?"

The rat elbowed the cat, who poked the dog,
who nudged the child.

So the farmer followed his wife, and his wife followed the child, and the child followed the dog, who followed the cat, who followed the rat—who was already wearing his napkin—down into the dell to eat the cheese.

And then the farmer stopped.

"You know," he said. "If we're going to have a party, we really should have some apples from the orchard to eat with the cheese."

"Delightful idea," said his wife. "And I'll fetch a few pears."

"I'll get the crackers," added the child.

The dog thought some sausages would be tasty as well.

And the cat insisted on milk.

So off went the farmer, and his wife, and the child, and the dog, and the cat to get some apples, and pears, and crackers, and sausages, and milk.

DOLL RULES
FARMER, FARMER party!

Everyone left the cheese alone except . . . you know who.

Take your time. I'll just stay here and hang out with the cheddar. Heh. Heh. Heh.

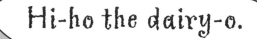

The farmer in the dell
The farmer in the dell
Hi-ho the dairy-o
The farmer in the dell

The farmer takes a wife
The farmer takes a wife
Hi-ho the dairy-o
The farmer takes a wife

The wife takes a child
The wife takes a child
Hi-ho the dairy-o
The wife takes a child

The child takes a dog
The child takes a dog
Hi-ho the dairy-o
The child takes a dog

The dog takes a cat
The dog takes a cat
Hi-ho the dairy-o
The dog takes a cat

The cat takes a rat
The cat takes a rat
Hi-ho the dairy-o
The cat takes a rat

The rat takes the cheese
The rat takes the cheese
Hi-ho the dairy-o
The rat takes the cheese

The cheese stands alone
The cheese stands alone
Hi-ho the dairy-o
The cheese stands alone

To my big
cheese—M.P.

The Cheese
Text copyright © 2007 by Margie Palatini
Illustrations copyright © 2007
by Steve Johnson and Lou Fancher
Manufactured in China.
All rights reserved. No part of this book may be used or
reproduced in any manner whatsoever without written permission
except in the case of brief quotations embodied in critical articles
and reviews. For information address HarperCollins Children's Books,
a division of HarperCollins Publishers, 1350 Avenue of the Americas,
New York, NY 10019.
www.harpercollinschildrens.com
Library of Congress Cataloging-in-Publication Data is available.
ISBN-10: 0-06-052630-0 (trade bdg.) — ISBN-13: 978-0-06-052630-6
(trade bdg.)
ISBN-10: 0-06-052631-9 (lib. bdg.) — ISBN-13: 978-0-06-052631-3
(lib. bdg.)

Design by Lou Fancher
1 2 3 4 5 6 7 8 9 10
❖
First Edition